QUIET DOWN, LOUD TOWN!

BY ALASTAIR HEIM

ILLUSTRATED BY MATT HUNT

FOR MOM AND DAD AND BROTHER E....
MY LOUD AND FUNNY FAMILY —A.H.

FOR MAXWELL —M.H.

Clarion Books
3 Park Avenue
New York, New York 10016

Text copyright © 2020 by Alastair Heim
Illustrations copyright © 2020 by Matt Hunt

Clarion Books is an imprint of Houghton Mifflin
Harcourt Publishing Company.

hmhbooks.com

The illustrations in this book were done in mixed media.

The main text was hand-lettered by Matt Hunt.

Library of Congress Cataloging-in-Publication Data

Names: Heim, Alastair, author. | Hunt, Matt, 1988– illustrator. Title: Quiet down,
loud town! / by Alastair Heim ; illustrated by Matt Hunt.
Description: Boston : Clarion Books/Houghton Mifflin Harcourt, [2020] | Audience:
Ages 4 to 7 | Audience: Grades K–1 | Summary: Mr. Elephant wants nothing more
than some peace and quiet—that is, until he gets it.
Identifiers: LCCN 2019038063 (print) | LCCN 2019038064 (ebook) | ISBN
9781328957825 (hardcover) | ISBN 9780358378556 (ebook) Subjects: CYAC:
Stories in rhyme. | Noise—Fiction. | City and town life—Fiction. | Humorous stories.
Classification: LCC PZ8.3.H41336 Qu 2020 (print) | LCC PZ8.3.H41336 (ebook) |
DDC [E]—dc23
LC record available at https://lccn.loc.gov/2019038063
LC ebook record available at https://lccn.loc.gov/2019038064

Manufactured in China
SCP 10 9 8 7 6 5 4 3 2 1

4500803617

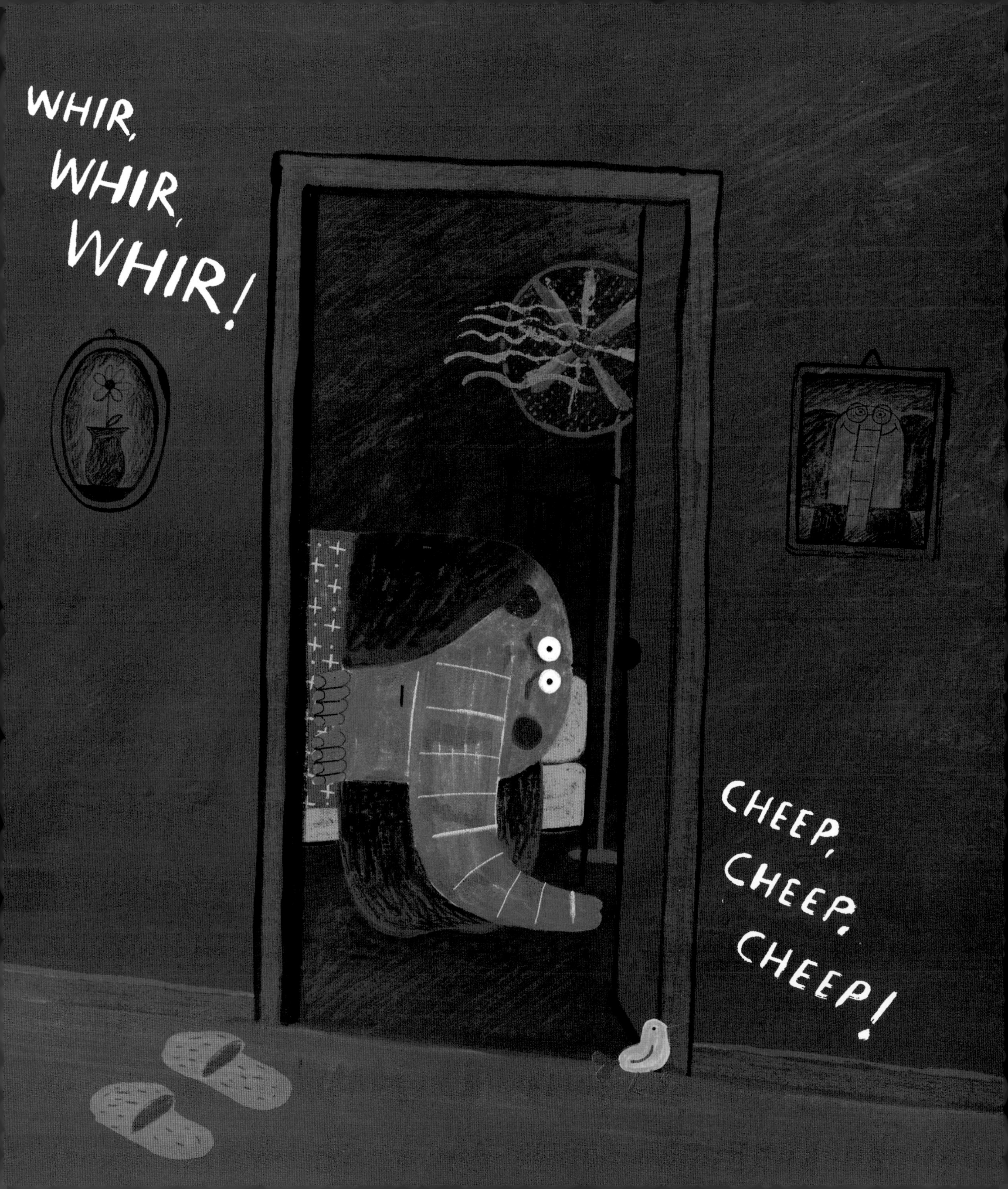
WHIR,
WHIR,
WHIR!
CHEEP,
CHEEP,
CHEEP!

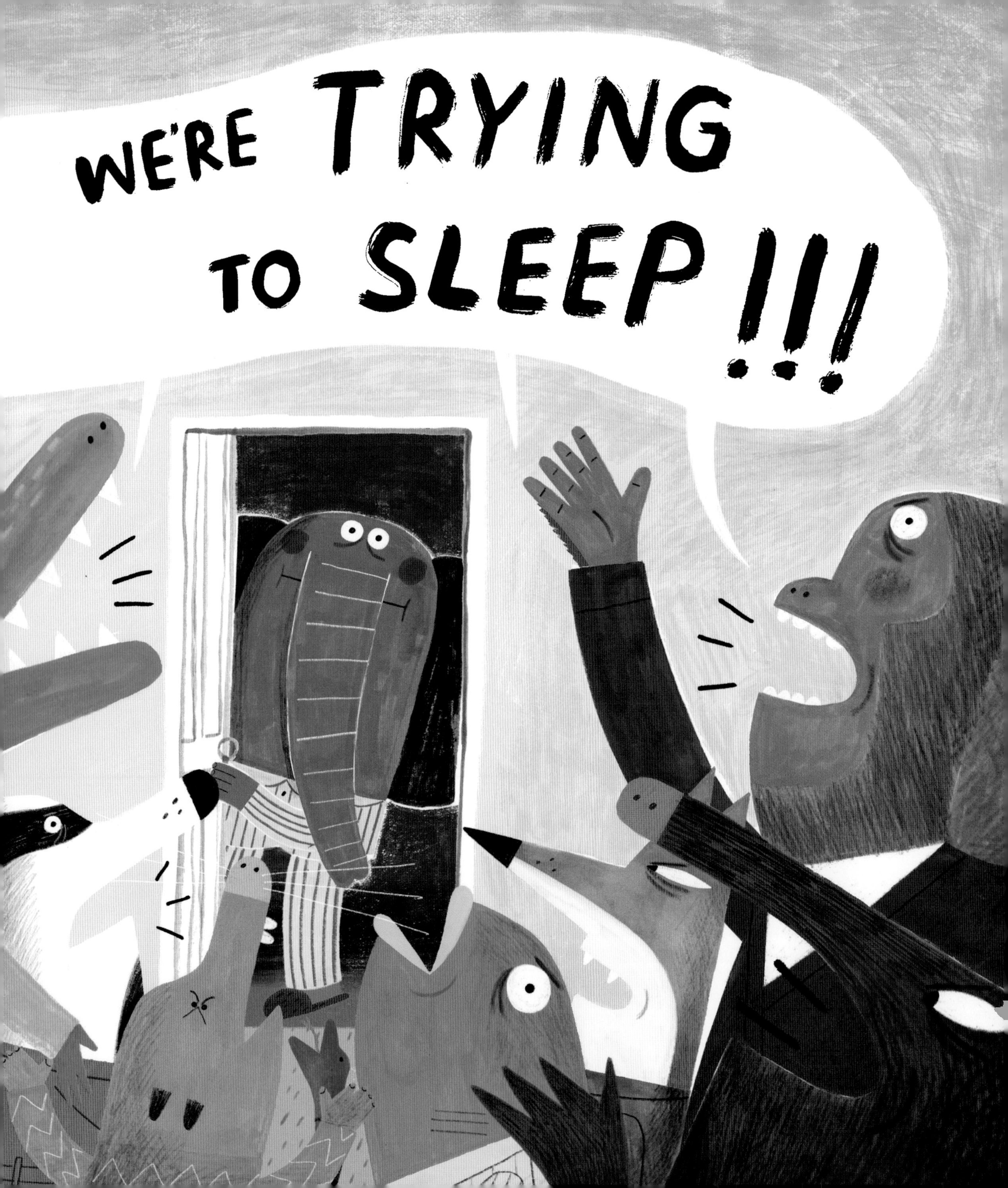
WE'RE TRYING TO SLEEP!!!